A Tale of Two Christmases

There are so many people to whom I owe a debt of gratitude. I have been so extremely lucky to be surrounded by family and friends who have supported and encouraged me.

To everyone who reads this little book, I hope you find something that you enjoy.

From me and all my very patient family, I wish you a very Happy Christmas and a Fabulous New Year to come. Love. Debbie xx

1.

Moll's Christmas

The shopping bag was heavy, and she had made the journey home harder by taking a wrong turn. She was still learning her way around the new neighbourhood. The rain began as drizzle, but fell harder with every footstep.

Her tears fell along with the rain, and she fumbled with the key. She swore quietly under her breath and shoved the door with her shoulder. Inside, finally out of the rain, she shook the bunch of keys in her hand loose, and tried one in the door to her flat.

"Are you alright? Oh my, you're soaked to the skin." The lady from across the hallway had knocked on the door to introduce herself on the day that they had moved in, but Moll could not remember her name.

"Yes. No. I got soaked in the rain." Tears slipped down her cheek.

"Why don't we find you something dry and warm to put on and have a cup of tea? You will feel better and we can get to know each other." She tucked her keys into her pocket and pulled her door closed. "I am certain that you have forgotten, but my name is Eileen. Your name, I remember, is Molly. There we go. We are off to a good start." She pushed Moll gently into the flat. "You change and I will make the tea."

Back in the kitchen in dry clothes, she found Eileen had made tea and unpacked the shopping. "That's better. Now, is everything alright?"

"Yes. It's just that this is all new. We thought moving to a new place would help." Another tear slipped loose. "Sorry."

"No apologies for tears, love. They are perfectly natural. Can you tell me why you are so sad?" Eileen sipped from her tea.

"Christmas. It's our first Christmas without my mum. First things are always hard. Her birthday was just after she died. But Christmas was always her thing. She made the crispiest potatoes, the best turkey. Planned for months. Now it's just us. I have no idea what to do." Moll reached for her cup. "Thank you for making tea."

"You're welcome." She smiled. "Christmas is only one day." Her eyes fluttered closed.

"Do you have children?" Moll leaned her elbows on the table.

"I have a daughter, Carrie." She smiled the tight smile she used to disguise her feelings.

"Is she coming to you for Christmas?" Moll's wistful

tone told the story of the mother she missed.

"No. She is going to the Maldives." Eileen sniffed. "I have upset her again. She is easy to upset." She folded the tea towel and ran her hand over it.

"I am sorry, and here I am moaning about Christmas." She reached across to Eileen.

"Not at all. You lost your mum. That's so sad." Eileen patted her hand. "She must have been a good mum for you to miss her so much."

"That's the problem. I thought she would be here to help me. She was always there. Last Christmas it was all just as usual. Too much food and lovely presents. Jamie fell asleep in front of the television and we cleared up. It was the same as every Christmas, right up until she told me that it would be her last." Her tears started up again. "I desperately wanted her to be wrong. Wanted the doctors to be wrong, but they weren't." She wiped her fingers under her eyes.

"That is so very sad. I am so sorry. It is a hard time when you lose someone you love." Eileen reached across for her hand. "You know what, though? Perhaps we could make some new traditions. There are eight apartments in this block. Some of them might be going to family or whatever, but those who will be here, we could share Christmas. They would bring their traditions, you bring yours. What do you think?"

"We could set up tables in the hallway. Maybe everyone could bring some food, and share. That could be such a lovely way to get to know everyone, too." She rested a hand on her belly. "I have so much I wish I could share with my mum."

"Would she have been a granny, or a grandma?" Eileen huffed out a laugh. "I always hoped to be a grandma one day."

"We could invite your daughter. Maybe ask her to cancel the Maldives and come for dinner here with her mum." Moll grabbed Eileen's hands. "She's lucky to have you."

"I'll drop a note through all the doors and see what they think, then we can decide." She patted Moll's hands. "When is the baby due?"

"Not until March. She would have been a great granny, but I'll have to manage without her. That's more scary than Christmas." She laughed, but there was no humour in it.

2.

Eileen

She opened the door into her flat and closed it behind her. Moll had been so upset. Maybe she had been able to reassure her a little. She hoped so.

Back in her comfortable armchair, she reflected on the conversation, and realised that it was the only one recently. When was the last time she had sat down with someone and talked? Slowly, she shook her head. That girl across the hallway needed a good Christmas. Eileen closed her eyes. Why was it hard to admit, even to herself, that she needed the same?

A new feeling, a surge of determination, pushed her from the chair. She opened the cupboard in her living room and pulled out a pad of writing paper and a pack of envelopes. She began to write. After three attempts, she had what she thought was a straightforward message, which she copied out until she had six sheets of paper. She realised, only then, that she did not know her neighbour's names. Eileen chewed her lower lip. Her clear handwriting marked the front of each envelope. 'Dear Neighbour.' Satisfied with her handiwork, she tucked the envelopes into the pocket of her cardigan and climbed the stairs.

Back in her own flat, she discovered that she was feeling better, perhaps happier. Maybe planning this meal for Christmas was helping her as much as her lovely neighbour.

Eileen took a look at the clock and dialled the number that she had been thinking of ringing for the last few days. When the voicemail message kicked in, she made a face. "Hello Carrie. It's mum. I know I upset you, and I'm sorry. Please, can we talk about it? I love you." She ended the call and wrapped her hands around the phone. It was done.

Eileen closed her eyes and nodded her head, falling fast asleep, only to be woken half an hour later by a knock on the door.

"Hello?" The woman on her doorstep had the most beautiful eyes she had ever seen. Deep dark brown pools in an almond-shaped eyelid. For a moment, Eileen was transfixed.

"Thank you for your invitation, but we are not Christian. We do not celebrate Christmas." Her voice was low, and Eileen struggled to hear.

"It's a meal. No religion involved, dear. It's up to you, but it would be a chance to get to know everyone in the building." Eileen smiled. "Would you like to come in?" She opened the door wider.

"I have to collect the children from school. I will think about it. Thank you for inviting us." She turned away.

Eileen lifted her hand to wave, but the woman was already nearly out of the building. She had started something. It felt good to be at the start of something new.

3.

Farzana

The walk to the school was short, but the rain was heavy and her coat was no protection from the thin dribbles which found their way inside. The note from the old lady had caught her by surprise. It had been a long time since she had been invited anywhere. The children were invited to parties of school friends, of course. The endless round of birthdays and gifts to be found was exhausting the tiny amount of money that she had. Her husband sent enough to cover the rent, and if she was careful, they had enough to eat. There was very little left over after that.

Thoughts of her husband were uncomfortable. She was honest enough to say that she did not miss his company. Their marriage had been for the benefit of their family pride. Nothing to do with the two of them, really. Her husband, having done his duty and produced two children, was now happily living with his boyfriend. She had no idea if the family knew and cared less. She was happy to be left alone with her children. A little more cash would have been helpful, but life was not so terrible.

She stood back from the crowd of mums waiting for the children to come out and felt her heart lift when they ran towards her. Their smiles lifted her heart and found a smile she had forgotten was there on her face.

The excited chatter about their day and the things that they had learned took them halfway home. Perhaps they would enjoy the meal. She took a breath. "We have been invited to have dinner with everyone at the building. It's on Christmas Day. Would you like to do that?"

The children turned to stare at her. Perhaps she had let them down by even thinking about it.

"Yes please. It would be so much fun." Sayed, her beautiful son, so wise beyond his years. "Would everyone in the building go?"

"Here is the invitation. Have a look." She pulled the envelope from her pocket and passed it to him.

"I think we should go." Her daughter's eyes turned towards her. "We have lived here for a long time and we have no friends in the building. Yes, please. I would like to go." Jayshree skipped up the steps to the front door. "Perhaps we should knock on Mrs Eileen's door and accept."

Farzana slipped the key into the lock and nodded. The children were right. Why not go? She knocked gently on the door and waited for Eileen to open up. "We have talked about it, and we would love to come to your Christmas dinner. I don't cook English food, but I could bring a dish that my family enjoys. Would that be acceptable?"

"That would be wonderful. May I ask your names? I am Eileen." She smiled down into the faces of the children.

"I am Farzana. This is my son Sayed, and my daughter Jayshree. Thank you for inviting us."

"I am so pleased that you will be coming. What beautiful names. I am very glad to meet you." Eileen rested a hand on each of the children's shoulders. "Would you like a cup of tea?" The children turned to their mother; their eyes hopeful.

"That would be very kind, if you are sure that we are not stopping you from doing something." Farzana smiled.

"Come in, I will put on the kettle." Eileen held open the door and stepped backwards, thinking that she had been a fool not to speak to her neighbours earlier.

4.

Andrew

The knock at the door surprised Eileen. She was enjoying her afternoon cup of tea with her new friend Farzana and the two children. She excused herself and opened the door.

"Hello?" The young man on the doorstep smiled broadly at her.

"Thank you so much for the invitation." His soft Scottish accent reminding her of a holiday years before when she had toured the glens and highlands on a coach. "I had hoped to go home for Christmas, but I have to work all the way through, so I had thought I would be spending Christmas alone. I would be happy to join you and meet my neighbours. It's a lovely idea. Thank you."

"Wonderful news. I'm Eileen." She held out her hand and found it grasped in his firm grip.

"Andrew. Good to meet you." He took a breath. "I'm not much of a cook, but I could bring some wine, some chocolates perhaps? Would that be alright?"

"I think that is a lovely idea. You're in number three, I believe?" He nodded. "Do you know your neighbours in number four?" He shook his head. "Ah, well then, you had better come in, as they are having a cup of tea with me, and you can meet them." She pushed the door open, and he followed her inside.

"Farzana, Syed and Jayshree? This is your neighbour, Andrew." She watched his eyes fasten on Farzana and his pale skin burn with a blush. "Do take a seat, Andrew. I will make you a cup of tea."

"Thank you, Eileen, you're very kind." He stumbled over the words. "Lovely to meet you, Farzana." He stretched to shake her hand. "Sayed, Jayshree."

Here she was, the woman he had wanted to meet for the last seven months since he had moved in and caught tantalising glimpses of her. Those beautiful eyes, the graceful way she moved. To begin with, he had assumed that she must be married, but he had been overjoyed to see no husband lived with her. She seemed so entirely unapproachable, yet here she was sitting smiling at him and he was to have Christmas dinner with her and her children. He

A TALE OF TWO CHRISTMASES

could not have been any happier.

"So, tell us, Andrew, what do you do for a living?" Here was the question he hated, delivered by Eileen with a smile and a cup of tea.

"I work for the council. Very boring." It was a stretch of the truth. His work was partly funded by the council, but telling people outright that he worked for the housing benefit department had lost him the chance of friendships before.

"Not at all. Very important to keep everything going. My husband spent five very happy years working at the town hall. That was long before your time, of course." Eileen smiled across at the young man.

They finished their tea and Farzana announced that the children needed to do their homework, to a chorus of groans. Andrew made his excuses, and they left together. His eyes never strayed from Farzana. Today had surely been his luckiest of all lucky days.

"So, what is Santa bringing for you two?" He focused on the children while they climbed the stairs.

"We don't have presents at Christmas." Sayed informed him, with his huge solemn eyes open wide. "We don't believe in Santa."

"Ah well, perhaps the question is, does Santa believe in you?" Andrew laughed as both the children turned to look at him with wide eyes and open mouths. "We will have to wait and see if he does, won't we?" The children turned to look at each other and then back at their mother.

She smiled down at their faces. "Homework. We do believe in that." She opened the door to their flat. "It was lovely to meet you, Andrew." The children rushed inside and she turned to him with her hand on the key and the door open. "I am on my own with the children, and my finances are stretched, to say the least. I really don't have money to buy Christmas gifts for them as well." Her eyes were downcast with what he imagined might be shame.

"Do you have a moment?" She looked over her shoulder at her children and pulled the door a little closer. "I mean no disrespect. I work for the council in the housing benefit department. If your finances are stretched, then you might think about applying for benefits." He shrugged. "You may be entitled to some help."

"We need no charity, thank you." Her voice was stiff with embarrassment.

"It isn't charity." He stood his ground. She lifted her eyes to his. "I could help you with the forms, if you would like?"

"I know you mean well." She took a breath, imagining all the things that she wanted to do for her children but could not. "Thank you, Andrew. I don't mean to be rude. I am just not used to people offering help. Thank you. It would be generous of you to help me with the forms."

"No problem. I will bring them home tomorrow. Perhaps we can sit together and fill them in?" He smiled across the gap.

"Can you come over after the children are in bed? I don't want them to know." She hung her head.

"Of course, this is just between us." He smiled, and carried the warmth of her smile and the hope in her eyes back into his flat. There he wrapped it in hope and every Christmas wish he had ever made.

5.

Gertie

She had been in a really bad mood all day. The tap was dripping again in the kitchen. She had been hoping that there would be something on the television that she would enjoy, but there had been nothing to her taste. The hands on the clock crept slowly around towards eleven. Perhaps a cup of tea would cheer her up. Although she was not hopeful.

The envelope caught her attention when she went to make a cup of tea. It could have been there earlier, perhaps. The bend and stretch to pick it up was difficult, but she managed it and ran her finger under the flap.

A Christmas meal, with a group of people she managed to avoid all year, sounded as much fun as her dripping tap. She laughed at her own joke.

The tea steamed in front of her while she read the note again. What would she be doing at Christmas? She had turned down several offers of marriage in her youth, believing that the right one would come along. Her work as a teacher has kept her busy, and she was content with her own company. It had only

A TALE OF TWO CHRISTMASES

been for the last few years when she had begun to wonder whether she had misjudged life. She still had books to read, but her sight was not as good as it once has been. She sipped from the cup. It might be interesting to meet the neighbours. If she hated it, she only had to come home.

It said that everyone might like to contribute a plate of food to share with the rest. It had been a while since she had cooked anything but ready meals. Perhaps she could buy something ready-made? Or pre-prepared? Yes, that would work. She would go. She shuffled herself to the door and out into the hallway, tucking her keys into the pocket in her skirt.

"Hello?" The woman had said she was in Flat 2.

"Hello." The door opened wide.

"I live in the garden flat. I received your note. Thank you for inviting me. I would love to come." She leaned against the door frame for support. "I'm Gertie."

"I'm Eileen. Would you like to come in and have a sit down for a minute?" She pushed the door even wider and Gertie shuffled inside.

"Thank you. I am a little tired." She sat heavily on the sofa, hoping that she would be able to escape from the squashy cushions when the time came. "Oooof." She huffed.

"I was about to make tea. Would you like a cup?"

Gertie agreed and they settled to chat. They were of a similar age and discovered that they had lived within a few streets of each other for more than forty years. "Which school did you teach at?"

"Everson Primary. I worked there for more than twenty years. I was Deputy Head when I retired." Gertie smiled at the memory.

"Oh my, you might have taught my daughter. Carrie Doherty." Eileen sat forward in her seat.

Carrie? No, I remember a Caroline Doherty. I believe there was a Michael Doherty too." Gertie closed her eyes in an effort to remember.

"Yes, Carrie is short for Caroline. What a small world. How lovely that you remembered her." They were both surprised when they discovered that they had spent two happy hours together, and agreed to get together again soon.

Gertie eased herself from the sofa and shuffled back to her flat. Her thoughts were in turmoil. She remembered Carrie Doherty for all the wrong reasons. Gertie only hoped that she had learned to be a better person. She had been a thoroughly nasty child.

6.

Jamie

His drive home was the usual mixture of too many cars and the radio playing some really cheesy Christmas songs. It was not his favourite time of year. He had gone along with the way Moll's family celebrated because it made her happy. If he was honest about it, he had missed the quiet, lazy way his family spent Christmas. He had been looking forward to not having the forced enjoyment and screaming.

But Moll was so sad. There was nothing he could do to help. When she cried, part of his mind spiralled into panic. He did his best to be supportive, to help her. He was not, however, what she needed.

It seemed, though, that the older woman who lived across the hallway had helped. She had given Moll something to plan.

He parked in their parking space and let himself in to the building and then to their flat. "Moll. Hi. How was your day?"

She was sitting cross-legged on the sofa, a pad on her knees. For the first time in such a long time, she was happy. He knew he would smile and go along with anything that made her happy again.

She showed him the note from Eileen and told him about all the neighbours. He knew he was being churlish. It would be good to meet the other people in the building. Christmas was as good a time as any to do it. "Are you hungry?" She followed him into the kitchen. "I think I nearly got it." She placed four roast potatoes on the plate in front of him and stood back.

He tasted. They all tasted like roast potatoes. That was, he knew, the wrong answer. He chose the third one. "That one is the best one." He said it with confidence.

"I thought so." She was so delighted. "They are pretty good, aren't they?" He watched her dance around the kitchen.

He wrapped his arms around her. "I'm looking forward to it." His lips grazed her jaw. She smiled up at him. His Moll was back.

7.

Jack and Ida

"Oh, look Jack, an invitation for Christmas dinner, with the neighbours. What do you think?" Ida pushed Eileen's note across the table.

"No, I don't think so." He straightened the newspaper he held up like a shield.

"Why?" She reached across and tweaked the top of the sports page.

"We wouldn't know anyone. It would be uncomfortable. Anyway, I'm not well enough." He shook his head. "It's really not possible."

"I think we should go. We could meet them, get to know them. We would only have to stay a little while." She could hear the wheedling tone creeping into her voice and disliked herself for it.

"Ida. You're being daft." He sighed, folding his paper. "This might be our last Christmas together."

"You said that last year, and the one before that. If it is, then it is. What it isn't is an excuse to stop living now." She picked up the cups and plates from breakfast, and cleared the table crossly, banging the plates into the sink.

He watched her stiff back, and he knew he was being unfair. She had always needed company more that he did. He had been selfish. "Alright then, we'll go. But we won't have to stay late." He laughed when she turned to smile at him. She was still the woman he had married forty-seven years before. She leaned across to kiss his cheek and let herself out of the flat to go and thank Eileen for her kind invitation.

"Hello? You sent us an invitation?" Ida was a little nervous.

"Yes. I'm running a little late this morning. The kettle has just boiled. Would you like a cup of tea? I'm Eileen, by the way." She stepped back into the hallway, and Ida followed her slowly.

"I'm Ida. My husband, Jack, he was a little nervous about coming because we don't know anyone. He's not very well." She accepted the steaming mug. "Thank you."

"Well, please tell him, none of us know each other, so we will all be in the same boat. I am sorry he has been unwell." Eileen sipped from her cup.

"Thank you." A tear slipped from Ida's eye. "Sorry. It's been a hard year."

"No need to apologise for tears. I've cried buckets in my life." Eileen smiled, resting her hand on Ida's. "I am so glad that you will be coming. That's everyone. The whole building. It's going to be great fun." She squeezed her fingers around Ida's.

"Yes, I think you're right." Ida said. "Jack is worried that he might get too tired and need to go early. If he does, nobody would be offended, would they?"

"Not at all. Please tell him to come and go as he pleases, and that I hope he will enjoy it." Eileen watched Ida's light steps take her back up the stairs. She had wanted to ask if Jack was better, to offer some help, but she had felt unable to. Perhaps once Christmas was over, she would know them well enough to have that conversation.

8.

Shopping and planning

Eileen had been up since the early morning, making lists. She had learned over the years that if she wanted things to go perfectly, then planning was the way to iron out any problems before they happened.

They would need to assemble the tables and chairs. There was no point in everyone cooking the same things. She would try to divide up the cooking as fairly as possible. She bit gently on her lower lip while she tried to work out what would be easiest for Molly to cook.

The shopping lists were long too. She took a breath. She would volunteer to cook the turkey. It was the most expensive thing on the list, and it seemed right that she should do that when she had invited everyone.

The phone rang, and she picked it up, hoping that it would not be someone trying to sell her something. "Hello?"

"Hello Mum. I got your message." Carrie's voice was flat. Her usual vigour seemed to be missing.

"I am so pleased that you phoned. I'm sorry I upset

you. It was unintentional, but it hurt you and that was wrong of me." Eileen forced herself to breathe normally. Apologising when she had no way to know what she had done wrong made her feel a little breathless.

"All forgotten." The words were clipped as they flew through the telephone to Eileen. "I might pop over during the weekend. We could have a cup of tea and catch up."

"That would be lovely. I'll make a cake." Eileen felt the weight of her daughter's anger lifting from her shoulders.

Saturday was damp and grey. Eileen was singing to herself while she made the cake, though. Old Christmas songs that she had thought were forgotten tripped from her lips while she mixed and stirred and baked.

When the doorbell rang, she greeted Carrie with a hug. Whilst it was not entirely reciprocated, at least she did not pull away. They sat down for tea and cake. Eileen had put out proper napkins and cake forks, and they ate together, sipping their tea.

"How have you been? It's lovely to have you here." Eileen could hear that her voice was twittering, but there was nothing that she could do about it.

"I've had a dreadful week. It has been hell. I am thinking about changing jobs. My so-called colleagues are driving me insane. They are so small-minded and bitter." Carrie's sharp eyes caught the deep breath that Eileen took.

"I'm sorry, love. Have you had a look for any jobs advertised?" Eileen straightened her back. This was not the first time that Carrie had fallen out with someone at work. Every job she took was short-lived. Someone would argue with her or take offence at a comment, and she would be back looking for a new post.

Eileen waved to her stiff-backed daughter. She wished that it was possible to help her to relax a little. Life would be better for her if she could.

9.

Not long to go

Andrew felt uncomfortable with what he had done. He had not broken any rules, of that he was certain. He had, however, processed Farzana's claim in record time. What should have taken six weeks had happened in three days. It was unheard of. The important thing, though, was that she would receive the money which would make her and the children's lives so much better.

Farzana had been overjoyed when she received the letter telling her that she would be receiving a regular payment to help her and the children. She had danced around the kitchen, small though it was. In return for all his help, she had offered to cook dinner for Andrew. He had accepted joyfully. It seemed that he was not a skilled cook, and the prospect of a home cooked dinner was the best thing she could have offered.

The children enjoyed their meal with Andrew. He told them jokes, and they shared their jokes with him. His voice was soft and gentle, and he laughed when they said silly things, and encouraged them to tell him all about themselves. Farzana watched him and imagined what life would have been like if someone like him had been her husband. Someone who was interested in the children, rather than viewing them as an inconvenient duty.

They studied the list together. Andrew was glad that his contribution was to be chocolates and wine. He had also bought a bottle of whisky, which was what his family would be drinking on Christmas day. Farzana was looking forward to trying all the English dishes and hoped that everyone would enjoy the dishes she planned to make.

While she washed the saucepans, the children brought him their letters to Santa. It was a new concept for them, but one that they were happy to adopt. Jayshree reasoned that as he worked for the government, he might be able to get their letters to Santa, when the post office, which their mother said was very unreliable, might not.

He took the letters solemnly and promised to ask his boss if it would be possible. Their eyes were huge, filled with imagining the possibilities that this might just work. "Don't forget to leave out something for Santa to eat, just a little something, and a glass of milk. He likes that." Andrew confided. "Probably best to leave it outside your front door, so that he can find it." They nodded and walked away together, arguing over what Santa might enjoy the most.

Back in his own flat, Andrew opened the letter they

had written together, expecting to find lists of toys and sweets. He was surprised and moved by what he found.

Dear Santa

We are new to this, so we hope that we have not asked for too much. Our mum is sad. Please, can you help her to be happy? She cries sometimes when she thinks we are watching television. Andrew is nice. He might need some new trousers. The lady downstairs is nice, too. She might like some tea bags. We would like some new socks each and some colouring pencils and paper.

Thank you very much.

Sayed and Jayshree

He found that for the first time in years, there were tears in his eyes. These children were wonderful. What kind of fool must their father be to walk away from them?

10.

Carrie

"Hello Carrie." Eileen stepped back from the door. Gertie had been making her way to Eileen's, but she decided to wait a moment, not wanting to intrude. There was a small seat in the hallway area and Gertie settled herself there to have a rest.

Carrie stepped inside the flat, leaving the door open, which seemed strange, but Gertie waited. She needed to get her breath back, anyway.

"I quit the job." Carrie's voice drifted out into the hallway. "They won't get someone as qualified as I am to fill the post. I have applied for several other posts. In fact, I had a phone call from one of them almost straight away. I'm certain to find something better in January."

"Oh my, they must have been very upset to see you go. Will it be alright, with your contract and all of that?" Eileen's voice sounded fluttery. Gertie despised herself for listening in, but was uneasy, hearing Eileen sounding so worried.

"For goodness' sake, mother. I am an adult, and I am perfectly capable of dealing with all of that sort of thing." Carrie's voice rose with irritation. "Please, just trust me to run my own life without your interference."

"Sorry. I was just concerned. I'm sure that you will be able to find something wonderful." Gertie shook her head. Eileen sounded so completely beaten.

"I will. There are so many vacancies now. People are leaving the profession in droves. It really was rather stupid of them not to treat me better." She sighed. "Well, it was only a flying visit. I just wanted to wish you a happy Christmas. I will be busy for the next few days, and I fly out on Christmas Eve, so I'll see you in the new year." The door pulled into the flat and Carrie left.

Gertie had heard no response from Eileen, but she imagined Carrie had not noticed. She shook her head. It appeared that nothing had changed since she was a very small child. She had been a bully then.

Her steps were slow but steady, and each one took her closer to her own flat. She wished that she had not overheard Carrie and Eileen, but wishing would change nothing. Gertie had been proud of her record as a teacher, but Carrie had been a failure. She had not managed to teach her to respect others. When she reached her own flat, she was glad to be able to sit down and have a few minutes to think of ways that she could help Eileen.

11.

Christmas Eve

The bubble of excitement settled just under Andrew's ribcage. He had phoned his mother, and chatted happily for half an hour. He now knew far more that he felt was strictly necessary, about every family member. His father had sent him Christmas wishes and his sister had shouted hello as she passed through the kitchen. He could see them all so clearly. But he would not swap the chance to have Christmas with his wonderful neighbours for a visit home. He finished work early and smuggled in the last of the presents he had been stowing carefully away in his wardrobe. His new trousers were neat and ready on a hanger. He had a little wrapping left to do, but it was nearly ready. His arrangements for the evening were all set.

Farzana had settled the children in front of the television. As a general rule, she tried to restrict their screen time, but they had been so excited, they all needed a break. The telephone rang. When her husband's name flashed on the screen, she stood still. "Hello."

"Farzana. Just wanted to let you know. I will be

A TALE OF TWO CHRISTMASES   33

calling in to speak to you tomorrow. I have received a letter saying that you are asking the government for charity. You know that I pay all your bills. There is no need for this at all. I have prepared a letter. You will sign it to undo all this nonsense." Had he always sounded so smug she wondered.

"Tomorrow is not convenient. I am taking the children to lunch with friends. Tomorrow is Christmas Day." She stood up a little straighter. Saying no to him was a new experience.

"I will be there to see you tomorrow. Make sure you are at home, or I will stop paying the bills and you will be out on the street. Do not imagine that I will hesitate." His voice was a hiss, low and dangerous.

"Fine. Do that. I will contact your mother and ask her for the dowry money back. There are rules. You cannot decide what happens to me anymore. I will not allow it. Don't come tomorrow." She ended the call, surprised at her own audacity.

Eileen checked that everything was ready. The tables were in place. Andrew and Jamie had set everything up. Molly and Farzana had laid the table, with her freshly ironed tablecloths and napkins. Gertie had provided the most beautiful glasses. Ida had fussed around them all, but had made them all laugh too. It had been such an enjoyable afternoon. The thought crossed her mind that Carrie would be flying soon, but she was too busy to dwell on it.

Molly kept checking the weather forecast. For weeks

they had been talking about whether it would snow. She so hoped that it would. Just a little bit of snow would make Christmas perfect. When the first flakes fell past the window, she squealed. "Jamie! It's snowing!"

They watched the flurries against the dark afternoon sky. Jamie draped his arm over her shoulders. "Happy?"

"Oh yes. It feels like a proper Christmas, doesn't it?" She smiled up at him, and she pointed to the cars. "Look, it's starting to settle." Outside their door, the children from upstairs shouted to each other, rushing out into the snow to dance and jump, catching the flakes on their tongues. Molly rested her hand on her belly. It was going to be alright.

When Sayed and Jayshree were back inside, tucked up in bed and fast asleep, Andrew tiptoed across the hallway and collected the two biscuits that they had left. He took a long drink from the glass of milk and piled presents against their door. He laughed to himself as he tiptoed back to his own door and whispered, as he had as a child. "One more sleep to Christmas."

12.

Christmas Day

The noise filtered through the building. Jayshree and Sayed had discovered that Santa had paid them a visit while they slept. Farzana watched them carry in the parcels and unwrap each new surprise with joy and squeals of delight. "We didn't ask for toys, though. I don't understand how this works." Sayed looked up at his mother.

"Wait, there's a letter!" Jayshree had discovered the heavy cream envelope between two parcels. "Oh my, look at this writing. It's beautiful." She turned the paper to show her mother and brother the calligraphy that filled the page.

Dear Sayed and Jayshree

Thank you for your letter. It was so kind of you to ask for presents for everyone else. I very rarely hear from children who want little for themselves. Your mother should be very proud of you. I thought you might like some things for you two, and I will work on the other things you asked for in your letter. Merry Christmas to you both. Love. Santa Claus.

The children looked at each other in wonder. "Can

we tell Andrew about this? He was the one who made sure that Santa got our letter." Farzana said it was too early, but a knock on the door proved her wrong.

"Happy Christmas! Do any of you know anything about these trousers? They were outside my door and they're a perfect fit." Andrew's puzzled expression had the children dissolving into giggles, and jumping with recognition that Santa had done as they asked.

"I think I should make some breakfast. Will you join us, Andrew?" Farzana escaped to the kitchen. Andrew followed. "I know that we have you to thank for these presents. You have been too kind." A tear slipped from her eye.

"No. Not nearly enough." He whispered. "I waited months for a chance to speak to the most beautiful woman I ever saw, and here I am in her kitchen. No presents could be enough." He watched her think about it, and slowly move her hand to rest next to his on the worktop. He moved his hand to cover hers. His smile filled his face, and hers when she raised her eyes to look into his was the same.

Eileen had been up early to put in the turkey. Her house filled with the scent of cooking and she hummed along with the radio while she basted the bird. Outside, the snow was several inches deep on the parked cars and the pavements. It all felt perfectly Christmassy. The knock on her door

A TALE OF TWO CHRISTMASES 37

brought a smile to her face. When she found it was Gertie, she was overjoyed. "Merry Christmas!" She opened her door and Gertie huffed her way to the sofa, passing a bag to Eileen. She opened it up and found boxes of mince pies, beautiful stollen, gingerbread and boxes of sweets. "Oh Gertie, this is fabulous." She laughed. "We will be eating all day!" She filled the kettle and made them a cup of tea. "The turkey is cooking. There is very little for me to do for a while. I'm so glad you came over." They settled down to chat. Eileen realised that she had missed having someone to talk to. Not that she had anything profound to say. Gertie felt the same. She had allowed herself to become too closed off from new people.

A knock on the door brought Molly and Jamie and good wishes for Christmas. Eileen checked the table again and basted the turkey. Jamie helped Molly to her feet before they went home to start peeling the vegetables.

"This was a good idea, Eileen. I am so glad that you invited me. Thank you." Gertie reached for Eileen's hands and held them tightly.

"Hello everyone!" Jack and Ida were surprised to be kissed and hugged by everyone, but they were glad to be made welcome. Andrew and Farzana seemed to be very happy in each other's company. The children were excited and noisy, just as they should be. Molly was fussing about the vegetables. There were piles of them on platters along the table. The turkey sat at the end of the table, golden brown and steaming hot. Farzana's dishes were spicy but not too hot. Gertie took a spoonful and declared herself a fan. The gravy and stuffing were passed along the table, and once everyone's plate held enough for a week, they started their dinner.

"This is wonderful." They said to each other. "I wish we had done this years ago."

"May I say something?" Jack raised an eyebrow. Everyone turned to him to hear what he had to say. "Thank you. For inviting us, for giving us this wonderful food, and better than that, for making us your friends. For years, I have wasted my time worrying about the bills and if it would rain. I wasted time that I could have spent with my lovely wife. Now we have less time ahead of us than we have behind us, and I wish I had not worried so much. I would like to propose a toast." He raised his glass of water. "To friendship." They all joined in the toast and drank.

The front door flew open, sending a cold blast of air into the hallway. "What is going on here?" Carrie stood on the doormat, her suitcase on wheels behind her.

"I thought you were in the Maldives." Eileen stood up.

"The flight was cancelled. This weather is dreadful." She stomped the snow from her boots. "Why are you having dinner with all these people? What is this, a

A TALE OF TWO CHRISTMASES

lonely hearts club?" She scoffed.

"These are my friends. You can sit down with us and have a Christmas dinner if you like." Eileen moved away from the table to fetch a chair.

"Eileen, she's capable of fetching her own chair, aren't you, Caroline?" Gertie fixed her with a glare. "She is also capable of being polite and friendly, I imagine." Gertie turned away and looked at the children. "What did you get for Christmas, Jayshree?" The chatter quickly returned to the previous level, leaving Carrie to decide whether she would join them or not, and Eileen standing next to the table.

Carrie marched into her mother's flat and returned with a chair. "I remember you. You taught me when I was very young. You were a cow then." There were gasps from the children.

"Yes, I was. We have that in common at least." Gertie watched the comment hit home. "Pass those wonderful potatoes, will you, Molly, dear?" Carrie thought about it and finally sat down at the table.

Molly passed the vegetables, and she watched Farzana with her children, and Eileen with Carrie. Her hand rested on her belly. She missed her mother, but she had found some comfort in the friends and the love that surrounded them in the building that they shared. Her mum would, she hoped, have been proud of her. The baby in her belly kicked hard against her hand. Maybe she had missed the point. Her mum had wanted this for her. A happy Christmas, and every day of the year. That was all everyone wanted for everyone they loved. A tear slipped from her eye, but it was a happy one. She turned to Jamie and smiled.

Merry Christmas everyone, and pass the potatoes!

13.

January

"Good morning, Eileen. I have always thought that January is a depressing month, after the excitement of Christmas, but this year seems different, don't you think?" Gertie huffed her way to Eileen's living room. The sharing of a morning cup of tea had become a habit, one that she was very much enjoying.

"You're right. This year has started well. Even Carrie is being pleasant." Eileen received a quizzical look from her friend. "Well, as pleasant as she gets." Eileen laughed.

The knock on the door was unexpected, but Eileen opened up. "Farzana, what a lovely surprise. Will you join us for a cup of tea?"

"Thank you. I wondered if you both might have some advice for me. I am worried." She crossed the threshold and sat down with Gertie, worrying at her sleeve while she waited for Eileen to bring them tea.

"Here's your tea. Now tell us what we can do." Eileen placed their cups carefully.

"It's Andrew. He's lovely." She smiled and they

both smiled back. "I have been seeing him since Christmas and we have been, well, you know." A blush coloured her neck and cheeks. "Which was fine. More than fine. Then my husband found out. He's furious and threatening to tell my family that I have been unfaithful to him. It would be a huge shame. They would be devastated." A single tear slipped from her eye at the thought. "He says if I stop seeing Andrew, he won't tell them." Another tear fell. "What do I do?"

"Why do your family not know that he is living elsewhere with another man?" Gertie tipped her head to one side to look into Farzana's face.

"I could not tell them. Where our families are concerned, well, they are very old-fashioned. It would hurt them. So, I kept it quiet. I suppose we both did." She took a breath to steady herself. "Now I am caught in my own lies."

"Yes. I suppose, but so is he." Eileen sat back against the cushions of the sofa. "If he tells your family, he would have to tell them why you are living alone, surely?"

"Yes, oh, yes, you're right. I shall remind him of that, perhaps. The thing is, I become entirely stupid when he starts shouting. It's as though my brain doesn't work anymore." Farzana shook her head.

Gertie shifted her weight uncomfortably.

"Are you unwell, Mrs Gertie?" Farzana leaned forward.

A TALE OF TWO CHRISTMASES 43

"Just stiff love. Too long sitting still, I think." Gertie smiled, but she was still uncomfortable.

"If you liked, I could show you some stretches, just simple ones, to help with that." Farzana raised an eyebrow.

"What sort of thing?" Gertie was intrigued.

"I have done yoga every day of my life since I was a child. It doesn't have to be difficult. I can show you." Farzana smiled. "I'd be happy to help."

"That would be very kind." Gertie smiled.

"Could I learn too?" Eileen asked. "We're definitely less supple than we used to be."

"Of course. It will be fun. How about now?" She laughed. "After we finish our tea"

14.

February

"It's nearly ten. I am so sorry I'm late. Everything is taking longer at the moment." Moll closed the door to her flat and joined the rest of them in the hallway. "I can't even walk straight. I'm waddling like a penguin."

"It will all be worth it when you hold that baby in your arms. Only a few weeks to go now." Farzana waited while Moll settled herself on the solid foam blocks and crossed her legs in front of her. "Right, let's start with some gentle stretches. Breathing in and out. Arms out to your sides, twisting gently through your body, bringing your arm over your head, and extending your hand out. Yes. Very nice." Farzana watched them all, gently moving their bodies and smiled. "Moll, are you alright?"

"Um, no. I think. Oh. I. That hurts." Moll rolled onto the floor."

"Let me help you, Moll." Farzana knelt by her friend and gently rubbed her back.

"Oh, my word, that's fantastic. What did you do?" Moll sighed.

"A little massage to relax the muscles. Your body is getting ready for the biggest, toughest work out ever. Sometimes things bunch up just to practice. You'll be fine. I'll help you to your sofa if you wish, or you can stay and watch the others? But your stretching is over for today." Farzana laughed.

Moll sat and watched the class stretch and bend themselves. Eileen had surprised them all by how easily she had found her way into the poses and stretches. Gertie had struggled to start with, but her health seemed to be improving with every week that went past. She had proudly announced that she and Eileen had also started walking around the block every afternoon. Ida had joined them and despite her belief that she would not be able to do any of it, she had surprised herself. It seemed to Moll, as she watched them all, that she had found a truly wonderful family just by moving into this small block of flats.

At the end of the class, when they all lay flat on their backs, listening to Farzana's gentle voice, their breathing deep and relaxed, Moll closed her eyes and breathed along with them. Each breath in taken together, and each breath out releasing the sadness they had held.

15.

March

Ida always did her shopping on a Thursday. She had always enjoyed the process, writing herself a list and walking around the supermarket. Today was a little more difficult because she was worried about Jack. He had been sleeping badly for the past few nights, and although it was her day to shop, she considered putting it off. She could just run to the local shop and top up on milk and bread to keep them going.

"Are you not going shopping, love?" Jack took a sip from his tea.

"I don't need to go today. I'll just pop down to the shop on the corner and get a few bits. There's plenty in the freezer." She took a bite from her toast.

"You always go to the supermarket on a Thursday. Why the change?" He raised his eyebrows.

"I'm not feeling like it today. Maybe tomorrow." She was avoiding the question, and he knew it. He shook his head and raised the newspaper to read it, rustling the paper crossly.

Ida knew very well that he was worried too, but she had tried to convince him to go to the doctor

A TALE OF TWO CHRISTMASES 47

without any success. All that happened was that he got angry, and she suspected that he felt worse.

With breakfast cleared away, she made sure that he was warm enough and comfortable in the living room and promised to only be half an hour before letting herself out of the flat and rushing down the stairs.

Eileen was in the hallway, just crossing to Moll's flat. "Good morning, Ida. How are you today?"

"I'm alright. Jack's not too good at the moment. Are you well?" She crossed the hallway to the main door.

"I'm fine. Sorry to hear that Jack's not been well. I'll pop up later for a visit if you think he would welcome the company?" The sound from Moll's flat stopped them both. "Oh my! She sounds as though she's in pain."

"She might be in labour. Is Jamie at home?" Ida knocked on the door. "Moll? Are you alright?"

The sound came again, a little louder.

"I'll go around the back. They might have left the garden door open." Ida slipped through the back door and into the garden, leaving Eileen to keep knocking on the front door.

"Moll? Can you get to the door, sweetheart?" Eileen lifted the letter flap. "Moll?" She almost fell over when the door opened and Ida stepped through to help her up.

Together they rushed through to the living room,

where Moll was on the floor cradling her belly. "Moll, love. It seems the baby has decided to arrive a little earlier than expected. I'll phone Jamie and an ambulance. Try to breathe through the pains." Ida scrolled through the numbers on her phone and dialled Jamie.

"Eileen? This is hurting. Is it supposed to hurt so much?" Tears slipped from Moll's eyes. "I don't think I can do this."

"Darling girl, everyone who has ever had a baby says the same. It hurts for a bit, but oh my, it's worth it. Once you have that little one in your arms, you will forget all about it. Come on now. We will practice that breathing that we read about. When the next contraction comes along, we are going to breathe through it together. OK?" Eileen wrapped her hand into Molls and gripped. "We're going to be fine."

"What if something is wrong?" Moll turned her head to Eileen.

"There is nothing wrong. It's natural, and frightening." Eileen felt Moll's fingers tighten as a contraction hit her and breathed with her to keep her as calm as she could.

"The ambulance is on the way. Jamie is leaving work and he'll get back as fast as he can. In the meantime, we need to keep Moll as calm and as comfortable as possible." Ida joined them on the floor as the contraction subsided.

"We should time how far apart the contractions are."

Eileen felt Moll's fingers tighten again. "Not too far apart, it would seem. Come on Moll. Breathe with me. Did your waters break, love?" Through the pain and the breathing, Moll managed a nod.

"Oh, oh, oh. I can't do this. Help me, Eileen. Another pain. Oh my god, how can there be so much pain?" She pushed herself away from the floor, coming up to all fours. "Oh! Eileen. I have to get this baby out. I can't cope anymore."

The doorbell rang, and Ida ran to let in the paramedics. "Thank god! She's almost back-to-back contractions."

"Hello, it's Moll isn't it?" The paramedic knelt on the floor. "Can I take a look?"

Eileen stepped out of the way, but held onto Moll's hand.

"Well, there we go. We aren't going to have time to get you to the hospital, love." Molly whimpered. "I need to feel for the umbilical cord before you start to push, so can you pant for me? Your friend can pant with you, just keep it going, until I tell you, alright?" The paramedic met Eileen's eyes over Moll's head and received a nod in reply.

"We are nearly there, Moll. The baby's head is nearly out. You are going to meet your little one anytime now." The paramedic's gentle voice was encouraging. "Alright love. Time to push. Give it everything you've got. Let's meet the person who has been causing all this trouble."

Moll pushed, sweated, cursed and nearly crushed the bones in Eileen's hand. When the baby arrived, she slipped gently into the hand of the waiting paramedic.

"Moll! You have a daughter. A beautiful baby girl." Eileen reached out and kissed Moll. "Take a look at her."

An angry cry from the baby lifted Moll's head. "She has something to say about it, I think."

"I'm going to get you both to the hospital to be checked out, but your daughter sounds perfectly well." The paramedic pushed to her feet. "I'll get a chair and a blanket to keep you warm and give you a minute to get to know your daughter."

Ida rushed into the room. "Please come quickly. My husband has collapsed. Hurry."

The two paramedics followed Ida up the stairs while Moll and Eileen listened to their hurried steps on the stairs, and marvelled at the perfection of the baby.

"I'll fetch a towel to wrap her in. We don't want her getting cold." Eileen stood up to go to the cupboard.

"Thank you, Eileen." Moll smiled.

"She needs to be warm." Eileen shrugged.

"Not for the towel. For being here." Moll turned her head to the side to smile across the room.

"I wouldn't have missed it for the world." Eileen smiled back and went to fetch the towel.

16.

April

Jack was sitting up in bed when Ida arrived in the ward.

"Hello love. How have you been?" She made herself comfortable in the chair next to her bed.

"I've been bored stupid. When are they going to let me go home? This place gives me the creeps. It's full of sick people." Jack shrugged. "I miss your cooking, too."

"Of course. They'll let you come home soon. Once you can climb the stairs, I suppose. I brought you in something to eat, so at least you can stop moaning about that." Ida tried to look fierce, but she missed it by a good distance.

"So, tell me again, it's all been a bit confusing. Why did they call the baby Ruby?" Jack settled back against the pillows and waited for the story.

"Because when they were in the ambulance, and you were wired up to every machine in the place, Moll asked the paramedics their names and they were Jane and Tanisha. Neither of them jumped out as names for the baby, so she asked what they were doing after work and they said their team members were going out for a curry. One of them made a joke about her nan calling a curry a Ruby. Apparently, it was rhyming slang in London. They explained it all to her, but by that time, the idea of the name had stuck. So, Ruby it is.

"I'm sorry, Ida." He reached for her hand. "I knew you were worried, but I ignored it. I just wanted it to go away."

"Silly old man." She smiled. "It was lucky the paramedics were there for Moll and Ruby. Jamie's pleased as punch with the little one. He spends all his time cuddling her."

"When I come home, I will spend all my time cuddling you." Jack laughed.

"Let's see you climb those stairs first." She patted his hand and watched him smile at her.

"Hello Jack. You're looking better. Ida says you'll be home soon." Eileen joined Ida at his bedside. "I brought you the paper in case you were bored."

"You're a good friend Eileen. Ida is a sensible person, but I am a fool. I should have listened to her." Jack's chin hit his chest.

"Obviously. But you won't make the same mistake again, so you aren't a complete fool, are you?" Eileen laughed and Jack lifted his head to first look surprised then to join in. "Also, you got to share an ambulance with our newest resident, little Miss

A TALE OF TWO CHRISTMASES

Ruby. I was glad Ida was there with us when she arrived."

"Ida said you were wonderful, so calm and patient." Jack smiled up at her.

"I don't know about that. I know she nearly broke every bone in my hand." Eileen laughed. "I'd never seen a baby born before. Except my Carrie and I was a little busy to appreciate the wonder of that birth." She smiled at them both. "Now, are you ready to go home, or shall I get a coffee and wait for you?" She looked at Ida.

"Go, Ida. You're wearing yourself out with coming to see me every day. I'll be fine and the doc said I can come home soon, so stop worrying." Jack held out his hands to his wife, and she leaned down to kiss him. "Love you." He whispered.

"Phone if you're bored. Or if you're not. Love you too." Ida kissed him tenderly and they left him to rest.

"He looks better." Eileen said as the swing doors closed behind them.

"Maybe, but he's not. The doctor didn't say he could come home." Ida sniffed. "They said he might never come home." A tear slipped down her cheek. One she had been holding in since talking to the doctor. "I'm going to lose him, and sooner rather than later, I think."

Eileen turned to gather Ida into her arms without

thinking. "Oh love. I am so sorry." She murmured into Ida's hair.

People passed them in the corridor and seemed to take no notice. Perhaps a good many people wanted to cry in a hospital and their friends wanted to offer them comfort. Maybe it was not such an unusual event. It was, however, the only time that Ida would have to come to terms with losing the man she had spent her life with.

17.

May

Andrew knew that today was the day. He had offered to take the children to school on his way to work, but Farzana had only smiled and assured him that she would be fine. She had kissed him, grateful for the offer.

His office window looked out over the high street where he watched people come and go and thought about how she would be coping. This was one part of her life where he felt excluded and where he was unable to help her. With a shake of his head, he went back to work and tried to concentrate.

When the buzzer went, Farzana was expecting it. "Hello?" He mumbled something, and she buzzed him in before opening the door to the flat.

"You're looking well." His smile was insincere, but perhaps he was trying.

"Come in. We need to sort this out. The kids are getting older and they know that you don't live here. When they talk to their grandparents on the phone, how are they supposed to answer when they are asked how you are? They don't know." She walked into the living room and waited for him to follow.

"I see them. They can tell the family about that. Dad's fine. We went to the park on Sunday and fed the ducks." He shrugged.

"I won't ask them to lie for you. It's unfair." She lifted her chin in defiance.

"That's fine. I'll stop paying for your bills then." The bitterness crept into his voice.

"I have sorted that out. The money you give us goes into two savings accounts, one for each of the children. I don't use it anymore." She smiled across at him. "I don't need your money, little though you give. What I want is my life back."

"What do you mean?" He looked genuinely startled.

"I mean, I want to tell the truth. You knew that you were attracted to men when we married, but you kept it a secret. Perhaps your family knew too. It was a mean thing to do. My family thinks we are living as a family. I don't think we have ever been that. I need to tell them. As you know, I have met someone, and he makes me happy, but more than that, the kids love him. Give them the chance to have a full-time father figure. Please." She watched his face for a reaction.

"What would you tell them?" It was a whisper.

"That you have found love elsewhere. It's true. What you tell them is up to you. That you have not lived here for two years and that we have decided to make that a permanent arrangement." She sat a little straighter in the chair.

"Will you marry him?" He asked.

"I have no idea, and no plans to. Perhaps one day." She admitted to him and to herself.

"I'll need to think about it. This has come out of the blue. You've changed since you met this man." He nodded, sure of his facts.

"Yes, I have. He makes me feel braver. You always made me feel less. I could have just phoned my parents, and yours, and told them. I am not asking your permission. I am giving you warning of my plans." She stood. The conversation was over.

"You've become a hard woman." He sneered at her.

"Yes, I have had to, haven't I?" She opened the front door and let him out, closing it behind him with a click.

Inside, she leaned against the closed door and took a long breath in and out. She checked her watch. She still had half an hour before the yoga class. Time enough to let Andrew know how it had gone.

Downstairs in the hallway, they were ready to begin. She looked at them all. How far they had come in the last few months. Ida was missing, but they had not expected to see her. She was spending much longer at the hospital lately, and they all knew that the day was coming when she would not need to go at all. The group of women who bent and stretched, who reached forward with their hands and lifted their faces to the ceiling would be there to support their friend when that day came.

18.

June

Gertie rarely used her walking stick anymore. She was much steadier on her feet, but she would take it with her today. They had arranged for a minibus to take them all, but there would still be a good deal of walking to be done. She checked her watch. It was nearly time to go.

They would meet at the front of the building and wait for Ida. That had been the arrangement. She pushed herself out of the chair and straightened her skirt. It would be better to be early than late.

Clearly, she was not the only one who thought so. Outside the building in solemn silence stood Eileen, Andrew and Farzana, Moll and Jamie. The hearse pulled up outside the building just as Ida walked out into the sunshine. The flowers on top of the coffin were beautiful. Soft waxy lilies and tiny white rosebuds splayed out through the greenery.

Ida walked to the hearse and laid her hand on the glass. A final touch, perhaps? Or courage for the day that lay ahead.

Nodding to the driver, she climbed into the minibus,

and the others followed her.

The service was short and filled with love and tender memories of Jack. A few friends who had known Jack for years came along, but made their excuses after the service, and the group were left alone again. They had all shed some tears through the service, despite the vicar's mumbled delivery.

"Shall we go home? We got some food in, just in case you were hungry." Eileen wrapped an arm around Ida's shoulders. She received a nod, and together they climbed into the minibus.

Back at the block, Eileen steered Ida to a chair in the hallway, and the rest of them brought out food and set up tables.

"May I say something?" Andrew broke the silence. The nods around the table told him that it was alright. "I met Jack on Christmas day last year. He told me three things that day. I'd like to share them with you, if you do not mind." He cleared his throat. "He said that he had lived a life filled with worry. He worried about everything, mostly because he thought he would let down Ida. He told me not to waste my time worrying about things I could not control. He told me that Ida was the only woman he had ever loved, and that if I could find someone half as wonderful as her, I should hold on to her with every bit of strength I could muster. The last thing he told me was that he had never drunk scotch whiskey before, and I was pleased to pour him a drink. He sipped and swallowed. He told me that he would like to try it again, just to be sure. We had laughed then, and whenever I visited Jack and Ida, I took him a 'check up taster', just to be sure." Andrew took a breath, too emotional to continue. "So, maybe this is the time to raise a glass to a true gentleman." He poured a little whiskey into each glass and passed them around the group. "To Jack." They raised their glasses.

"Thank you, Andrew. That was so kind. We never had any children, but I know that Jack thought of you as the son he never had. All of you have been such wonderful friends to both of us. You have given him the best six months he could have had at the end of his life." She wiped her hand across her face. "Oh my, that's enough now. Let's remember Jack the way he should be thought of. He was a wonderful man. He loved all of you, and this block. He knew he was going, and he wished you all well for the rest of your lives." She picked up a sausage roll. "This is very kind. "And really rather delicious." She smiled. "He'll leave a huge gap, but I have had time to think about this and I have decided to try to remember how lucky I have been to spend my life with him, rather than regret the time I won't have."

"Jack was a wonderful man. I will always be grateful to you for convincing him to come to Christmas dinner. Thank you for sharing him with us, Ida." Eileen raised her glass to Ida and the rest of the group raised theirs too.

19.

July

Carrie zapped her car to lock it and walked on spiky heels to the front door. She hit the buzzer with her sharp red nails. When it buzzed, she pushed through the door, and knocked on Eileen's door.

"Mum?" Carrie pulled herself up to the tallest that she could make herself. "I have something to tell you."

"Carrie. This is a surprise. Come on in. Would you like a cup of tea?" Eileen stood back to let Carrie inside.

"No, well, yes. But not for a minute. I need to tell you something first." She took a breath and held onto the back of one of the kitchen chairs. "Right. I'm, well, Richard and I have decided to make a go of things. We are moving in together."

"I didn't know you were seeing Richard again." Eileen raised her eyebrows but said nothing more.

"We managed to iron out our problems. Mostly me, it turns out. You know I was seeing a counsellor, and that has really helped. So, I bumped into Richard in March and we started talking. He had missed me, apparently. We are really happy. I hope you will be happy for us, too." She took a breath, as though she had run a mile.

"I am so happy for you. More than that. I'm so excited that you're happy. It has been wonderful to watch you find your happy space over the last few months. This calls for a celebration. Perhaps you could bring Richard round for dinner. Would you like that?" Eileen heard the tremor in her voice. It was taking her a while to relax with Carrie's new happiness, and she was still worried that she might lose her temper.

Carrie watched her mother across the table. "That would be really kind of you. Yes, I'm sure that would be fun. I'd love that cup of tea too, if it's still on offer." She slipped her jacket off and hung it on a chair. "I am sorry, you know. I know I was a mean, miserable human. It's been a hard few months confronting the way I was. I am so much happier." She sniffed. "I should stop by and thank Gertie, she started it all at the Christmas dinner." She smiled up at Eileen when a cup of tea arrived in front of her. "Thanks mum."

"You're very welcome, love. It would be lovely to sit down to dinner with both of you. We will have to arrange a day when you're both free." Eileen lifted her cup and took a sip.

"Ha! You're busier than me. This block is full to the brim with your friends. But yes, let's arrange it. I'm looking forward to it." Carrie raised her mug in a toast and clinked with Eileen.

20.

August

"Look at you! So clever! You're crawling, that's amazing." Moll clapped her hands and watched little Ruby pushing herself across the carpet.

"She's a bit wonderful, isn't she?" Jamie reached for Moll. "But then she has an amazing mum."

"Aww, now I know you're angling for something." Moll laughed. She laughed more recently, and he was happy to see the change in her.

"You're all I ever want." Jamie smiled. "Well, you and Ruby."

"Sweet." They watched their little girl trying to push herself a little further. "I think she's tiring herself out."

"She'll sleep well tonight. It will be nice to catch up with Andrew and Farzana. Kind of Eileen to babysit for this one, too." He reached for Moll's hand. "It'll be nice to be out as a couple again, too. Even if it's only upstairs." He laughed.

"And Farzana cooks like an angel. I am so looking forward to the dinner." Moll stepped towards him.

"You're a lovely man. Ruby's a lucky girl to have such a nice dad." She reached up and kissed him. "Date night!"

"Oh nice. Date night it is." He wrapped his arms around her and pulled her close to him. An angry squeal from Ruby took their attention. She had made her way to the sofa and had found that it was blocking her way.

"Is that bad sofa in your space, baby girl?" Moll picked her up and kissed her. "Right, I'm going to give this little one some dinner and a bath, then I can get ready and we will get to Farzana and Andrew's for dinner." She kissed Jamie.

"I'm hungry. What is madam Ruby having?" He followed them into the kitchen.

"Vegetable puree. Delicious." Moll slid Ruby into her high chair and passed her some toys to play with.

They knocked on Farzana's door only five minutes later than they had been aiming for.

"Hello, come on in. Oh, you brought wine, thank you. Wonderful friends. I have always said that about you." Andrew smiled widely and pulled Moll into a hug. He shook Jamie's hand and led them into the flat. The smell of dinner filled the space, and they breathed it in.

"Wow, something smells amazing." Jamie smiled. "How was your holiday?"

"Oh, we had a lovely time. Farzana and the children

were a little nervous about meeting my family, but my sister and my mother soon sorted that out. My dad had the kids out on the loch fishing before we had been there for an hour. My mum fed us all as though we hadn't eaten for a month." He gestured to the table. "Shall we sit down?"

"Moll, Jamie, how lovely to see you." Farzana wrapped them in warm hugs. "I hope you're hungry." She joined them at the table and smiled up at Andrew when he poured the wine. "We had the best time in Scotland. It was beautiful. We walked up and down the mountains. And we went to a loch and a glen. It was wonderful, so beautiful."

"I'm so pleased. What did the kids think?" Moll helped herself to another mouthful of lamb that melted in her mouth.

"They have talked of nothing else since we came back. Their father was furious when he found out we had taken them, but there's nothing he can do." She leaned across to talk quietly to Moll. "A year ago, I would have been terrified by his anger, but I'm stronger now. I have friends here, and Andrew, of course."

"You do have friends. And so do we." Moll squeezed Farzana's hand. "And I for one, and so glad."

21.

September

"We are back at school now, but in a higher up class, Mrs Eileen." Sayed took one of the biscuits from the plate that he had been offered.

"How exciting. Now, come and tell me all about your holiday. I haven't had a chance to hear the stories yet." Eileen sat down on the sofa and smiled when Sayed climbed up next to her.

"Oh, I have so much to tell you. We met Andrew's mum and dad, and then his sister and her family. Andrew's mum and dad are called Mara and Gordon. They were so nice. Mum was worried that they might not like her, but they laughed at that. We went out onto the loch which is Scottish for a big lake." He snuggled into her. "Of course, we told them about you, and Mrs Gertie, and about school. Gordon showed me how to catch fishes, and we brought them back for dinner. There was a thing called a glen, and I wasn't sure what that would be. We walked up a big hill with grass and sheep on it. Then at the top we looked down the steep sides, and that was the glen." He was almost breathless with it. "We are going back again soon. Gordon said I could go

A TALE OF TWO CHRISTMASES   69

fishing with him anytime." For the first time since he had started talking, he looked carefully at Eileen. "How have you been? Did you miss us?"

"Yes, I did. I am so glad that you had a lovely holiday, though." She smiled down at his excited face.

"When we were on the train coming home, Dad phoned and he was very angry. Mum went away from where we were sitting, but we could hear him shouting. She said it was all fine, but I know it really wasn't. Why would my dad be angry we went on holiday, Mrs Eileen?" He turned his face towards her, expecting an explanation.

Sayed's confusion worried Eileen, but what could she say to reassure him? "Well now, I am uncertain why. I don't know your dad, but perhaps he was cross that he didn't know before you left."

"That makes sense. This is why I like talking to you, Mrs Eileen. You explain things." He smiled, his normally happy personality restored.

"Well, thank you. Now, shall we see if there are any more biscuits in the kitchen?" Eileen pushed herself up out of the sofa and heard him bouncing along on the carpet behind her.

22.

October

"Mrs Gertie? Are you at home?" Jayshree knocked on the door to the garden flat. She heard someone coming to the door, and she smiled, waiting to see her friend.

"Jayshree? Is that you?" Gertie's voice came from just behind the door.

"Yes, Mrs Gertie. It's me." She jumped and waved her hand across the spyhole where she knew Gertie would be watching.

The door swung open and Gertie stood back to let Jayshree into the flat. "How lovely to have a visit from you."

"I had to come and see you. Mum said it would be alright, but I was to ask if you were busy and if I was disturbing you, then I was to go straight home." Jayshree's solemn eyes waited for permission.

"Of course I'm not busy. What can I do for you?" Gertie led the way to the sofa and patted the seat next to her. "Come and tell me about your day."

"I had a lovely day. The teacher was very pleased

with me. Those excruciating maths problems were back, but after the way you explained them to me, I got every single one right. I would never have been able to do that on my own, so thank you." Jayshree showed Gertie the exercise book she had brought with her.

"Oh Jayshree. I am so proud of you. You are wrong about one thing, though." Jayshree's eyes opened wide. "Nothing to worry about. You did the work. You got them right. Not me."

"Let's agree that we both did well!" Jayshree reached for Gertie's hand.

"Yes, lovely. Now tell me how it went with your English essay?" Gertie settled in for a long conversation. Jayshree was a joy. In all her years of teaching, Gertie had never met a child who loved to learn so much. All she needed was someone to explain things to her, and she absorbed it like a sponge.

"Oh, Mrs Gertie. The teacher loved my essay. I wrote seven pages, which was more than anyone else, and she said it was..." She thought about it for a moment. "Insightful."

"Your teacher is right. It's the perfect word for you. I think your writing is perfectly wonderful." Gertie patted Jayshree's hands. "Thank you for coming to tell me. You have made my day."

"Oh, and mum said to tell you that Ruby is crawling properly now. It's lovely to see her grow up. She's very cute." Jayshree chewed her lip a little.

"Was there something else that you wanted to ask me?" Gertie settled back and waited.

"Yes. But I don't know how to. I'm not certain that I got it right." Jayshree looked uncomfortable.

"I always think it's best to just jump in when you need to know something." Gertie smiled, leaving her young friend to make the decision.

"If my dad and my mum aren't friends anymore, but Andrew and my mum are friends, does that mean that I could have another brother or sister?" She shrugged. "I'm not sure if it works that way, or you have to be married."

"Well, with these things, you never know. Babies come when the time is right. There are no rules, really. Perhaps we should wait and see what happens." Jayshree smiled widely.

"Yes. That seems a sensible idea. Did you mind me asking?" Jayshree tipped her head to one side.

"Not at all. You can always ask me whatever you want. I do not guarantee to know the answer, but I will try my best." Gertie smiled.

The knock on the door was a surprise for both of them. Gertie pushed herself out of the sofa and went to check the spyhole. She turned to Jayshree. "It's your mum." She opened the door. "Hello, Farzana. Come on in."

"Thank you so much, I hope Jayshree has not been

taking up your time." Farzana waited next to the door.

"She and I always have so much to talk about, and I am grateful that she comes to see me. She is a bright spark." Gertie patted Jayshree on the shoulder as she skipped to the door.

"You're very kind. She needs to do her homework, but we are hugely grateful for your help with her mathematics." Farzana's smile lit her face.

"Call by anytime." Gertie waved from the door. She closed the door and smiled to herself. Not for the first time recently, she realised that she was happy. She had new friends and lovely children upstairs who came to visit her to tell her about their day. Life was better. In fact, life was wonderful.

23.

November

"Eileen? Are you at home?" Moll had Ruby on one hip and a smile on her face.

"Moll? How lovely. Come on in. You're right on time. Hello little Ruby, are you going to help us?" The baby gurgled her delight and smiled up into Eileen's face.

"I am so excited about this year. After last Christmas, I think everyone is." Moll followed Eileen into the living room and gently lowered Ruby onto the floor. "Even Jamie's excited." She laughed.

"I think Carrie might come for Christmas dinner, and bring her partner Richard. I wondered if that would be alright with everyone. I know she turned up last year and it was all a bit last minute, but perhaps I'll ask everyone if they mind." Eileen studied her hands. "Carrie has not always been an easy person. Her dad died when she was young, and that didn't help. Honestly, though, I spoiled her. It was my fault. She's been seeing a counsellor, and it seems to be helping."

"I cannot imagine anyone would mind. Perhaps there would be others who might invite family. We could ask. In the meantime, we need to plan who is doing what for the meal." Moll smiled across the room. "I might ask Jamie if his parents would like to come." She laughed. "We could need more tables."

"We might." Eileen agreed. The doorbell rang. "Hold on."

Gertie joined them in the living room. "Hello Moll. Hello little Ruby." She shook her head. "Can you believe a year has gone past since we last planned a Christmas dinner?" She smiled. "It will be your first Christmas, Ruby. How exciting."

They sat and discussed the meal and the crackers, and who might like to make what. They talked about Ida, and how she would be about her first Christmas without Jack. It was a happy afternoon, and one spent with tea and laughter, and a few tears.

Another knock on the door had Eileen on her feet again. "Hello Andrew, how lovely. Come on in."

"I'm sorry to disturb you. I knew that you were meeting today, and I wanted to ask for some advice." He stood in the doorway, shifting his weight from one foot to the other.

"Come in, Andrew. How can we help?" Eileen offered him a seat.

"The thing is...you know about Farzana and me. I love her. I wanted to ask her to marry me. I know she's still married but, something that makes it feel more permanent, to tell her how I feel." He chewed his lip. "What do you think? Will she laugh in my face?"

"I cannot imagine she would do that. She's a gentle, sweet person. There's no cruelty in her." Moll reached for his hand. "She loves you as much as you love her."

"Oh, I don't imagine that I could be that lucky. I'm new to this, but I bought a ring. Would you have a look and see if it's entirely the wrong thing?" He searched in his jacket pocket, and worry crossed his face while he patted all the pockets until he found the box he was looking for. "Here it is." He pulled the box out and snapped the lid open. "What do you think?"

"Oh my! That is absolutely beautiful. I'd marry you to get my hands on that ring." Gertie laughed.

"Do you think she would be likely to accept my proposal?" Andrew closed the lid and slid the box back into his pocket.

"I think she would, but the only way to find out is to ask her." Molly told him.

"OK. Now I just need to pluck up the courage to ask her. Thank you, ladies." He patted the pocket which held his hopeful question. "I'll leave you to it."

"Well, how exciting is that? We will have to see what happens. How lovely." Eileen sat back down in the armchair, and smiled across the room at her friends.

24.

December

As all adults know perfectly well, time, usually predictable and easily measured, speeds up, powering through the first twenty days of December, when they had imagined that there was plenty of time, throwing all plans and possibilities into disarray.

Of course, all children know that December is, in fact, the longest month of the year. The last few weeks of waiting for the big day felt like months.

The only person in the building who was entirely uninterested in Christmas was Ruby. Her smiles and her sleepy tears continued in the same way. She liked the tree and the twinkly lights, but as she was not allowed to touch it, the tree became more of a battleground than an excitement.

"We made pictures from glitter today in school. It was so much fun." Sayed jumped up the steps to the front door. "Did Gordon telephone today?"

"Not to me, but perhaps he called Andrew. We can ask him when he comes home." Farzana unlocked the door.

"Can we have a Christmas tree at home?" He hopped through under her arm.

"I don't know. Honestly, I hadn't thought of it. Would you like one?" She laughed, watching him dance about on the stairs.

"I would like a tree." Jayshree had been quiet on the way home.

"Would you? OK, let's see about getting one. How was your day?" Farzana climbed the stairs.

"It was alright. I wondered about what we were talking about yesterday." She saw her mother's head turn towards her. "I was thinking, perhaps we could invite your dad to Christmas dinner, and his friend?" Farzana took a breath. "What do you think?"

"I think he'd be surprised." Jayshree stopped at the top of the stairs. "Would Andrew mind? I wouldn't want him to be upset."

"I don't know. Shall we ask?" Farzana opened the door to the flat. "Come on, let's get your homework done and then we can talk to Andrew when he gets home."

On Christmas Eve, when the last present was wrapped and dinner with Gordon and Mara had been eaten and cleared away, and Jayshree and Sayed, who had come to Father Christmas later than most, had left out milk and mince pies, and gone to bed with excitement bubbling through their veins; Gordon and Mara went back to Andrew's flat, where they would be staying the night. Farzana knew that the children would be awake early, and began to get ready for bed. Andrew paced the floor. He had not yet been brave enough to ask her.

"Are you not coming to bed?" She asked.

"I am. But I wanted to ask you something. I have a present for you, and I can't wait until tomorrow. Please." She sat on the side of the bed and waited. "You see, I love you, Farzana. I want you to know how much. I'm getting this wrong. I know you're still married, but please, will you consider making what we have together permanent?" He reached into his pocket and pulled out the small box he had been carrying everywhere with him for the last month.

"What is it?" Her brows pushed together, and she opened the box slowly. "Oh, Andrew. How can this be?" She closed the box. "No. I can't marry you." Tears filled her eyes, and she saw his filling too. "No. I....was so unhappy when I was with my husband. Nothing would make less happy than to be owned by another man." A tear slipped from her eye. "I want to be unmarried, if anything."

"Do you not love me?" Andrew's stiff words filled the gap between them.

"You know I love you. But you're trying to put me in a box." She lifted the box he had given her. "This tiny box. Where I won't be able to breathe."

"No. I want nothing like that. I want you to be free, and be assured that I love you." He knelt on the floor in front of her. "So, how about I change the question? Will you wear my ring and be unmarried with me?"

She laughed. "Now that's an offer I like. Yes, please. I would like very much not to marry you. And the ring is too pretty to keep in a box." He took the ring from the box and slipped it onto her finger. "I love you, Andrew."

"Happy Christmas, Farzana." He wrapped his arms around her. "I love you too."

25.

Christmas Day

"Yes! It's Christmas. Can we go and wake Gordon and Mara?" Sayed jumped up and down next to the Christmas tree.

"Only if the hallway light is on. Remember?" Sayed crept across the hallway and peered through the frosted glass by the front door. He jumped when he found that Gordon was peering back at him.

"Good morning, Gordon!" Sayed jumped up and down. "Happy Christmas. Mum is making breakfast if you're hungry."

"Wonderful, we'll be right over." Gordon called.

Gordon and Mara arrived, dressed and hungry. They chatted over the table and passed around toast, eggs and bacon, and tomatoes. When the children were released to choose a present, Gordon leaned across the table.

"My eyesight may be failing, but I think you have something to tell us, if that ring is anything to go by, and perhaps those children should be calling us Gramps and Grannie? Or am I very much mistaken?" He sipped from his cup of tea.

"You aren't mistaken about the ring. Farzana has agreed to be happily unmarried with me until we are old and grey." Andrew laughed.

"In that case, we are family, and Sayed and Jayshree just got themselves some grandparents." Gordon reached for Farzana, and pulled her in for a hug. "You don't need a ring to be family. We just didn't want you to be pushy, but we love you and your kids." He stood back to see that she was smiling widely. "Welcome to the clan."

Andrew went down to help set up the tables while Farzana cooked their contribution. The voices from the living room, filled with excitement and gentle kindness, filled her eyes with tears and her heart with gratitude.

The table was set with pretty cloths and glass and crockery from every flat. The residents and their guests gathered together. Ida and her sister sat together. They had happy memories to share of Christmases spent with Jack. She made a point of touring the tables and hugging every single one of her neighbours and thanking them for being her friends for a year. Eileen sat with Richard and Carrie, a little awkwardly, in the way that strangers are. Moll watched Jamie and his parents playing with Ruby, and smiled. Her mother would have loved to watch the way all the residents were supporting each other. Gertie joined Eileen and her family. The tension was still there between her and Carrie, but they were both trying.

A TALE OF TWO CHRISTMASES 83

Andrew and Farzana sat with his parents. "Would you like some more potatoes, Gramps? They're really delicious." Sayed's clear voice rang out in a moment of quiet. The whole room turned to look at Farzana and Andrew.

Andrew stood up and smiled. "I would like to announce that Farzana and I are engaged not to be married. She has already tried marriage, and has two wonderful children as a result, but we are going to build our family in our own way. She has, however, agreed to wear my ring, and put up with me." Cheers rang out around the tables.

Farzana stood up. "I have something to say, too. Before you ask me, yes, the children already know what I am going to tell you, but Andrew does not, and neither do Gordon and Mora. Neither does my husband, or his partner, Joe." She pointed to the two men sitting with them. "So, I hope that you will all forgive me for telling you in public." There was a moment when she wondered why she was telling them all like this, but only a moment. All around the tables were her friends. Every single one of them had been a stranger a year ago. Yet here she was, surrounded by people she loved. "Andrew was right. We are building a family, us on this table, and all of us in this building. Like all families, we will lose members, like Jack, earlier this year. And we will have a new member soon." She held her hand on her stomach.

Andrew stood up next to her. "Farzana? Are you

sure?" She nodded and bit her lip. "Oh my. I have never, ever been so happy in my life." He wrapped his arms gently around her. "Thank you so much."

After a moment of shock, the room erupted with shouts of congratulations and excitement.

Gertie wrapped her arms around Jayshree and squeezed. "It looks as though you got your wish."

"I think, as far as I can work out, that this is what Christmas is. It's about hope and the chance of a new beginning." She hugged Gertie tightly.

"Merry Christmas to you, Jayshree, and to all of us. I think we have a wonderful year ahead of us. You're right, we have hope and a new start." Over the little girl's shoulder, Gertie's eyes met Ida's, and they shared a moment. Sadness, certainly, and the joy of being included in the hope for the future.

Printed in Great Britain
by Amazon